THE CARRYING CAPACITY OF PARADISE

DEBORAH L. DAVITT

LUNA NOVELLA #22

Luna Press
PUBLISHING

www.lunapresspublishing.com
ISBN-13: 978-1-915556-49-3

For my husband, Jason,
who gives me the freedom to fly.

Contents

Chapter One

The mountain at the centre of Rheasilvia crater on the asteroid 4 Vesta had never been named by astronomers. Somehow, the highest mountain in the solar system, a full twenty-two point five km from base to peak, had never been deemed worthy of its own cognomen. The residents of Vesta had opted to call it *Amalthea*, for the goat that had nourished infant Zeus, when his mother Rhea had been unable to do so.

Security Chief Liane Sheridan hovered in mid-air near that polar peak, the light of a distant sun condensed and refracted by satellites above to illuminate a region that would have rarely seen more than shadows. Above her, a wide, radiation-proof dome tented the entire crater, ethereal graphene struts anchored on the peak securing the whole thing under the effects of microgravity even as the man-made atmosphere created lift, belling out the dome like a balloon.

That atmosphere remained thin, generated by the robots that trundled from acre to acre, converting icy regolith to flinty soil, water vapour, and carbon dioxide, while spreading a host of useful cultivated bacteria in their wake. The trees, of course, took these resources and converted the carbon dioxide to breathable oxygen. Below her, sequoias lifted needle-laden branches towards the columns of sunlight streaming over the crater edge towards them. Freed from the constraints of gravity, conservative estimates suggested that these saplings, which already towered here, might grow a full kilometre in height.

Liane hoped she'd live long enough to see that happen. Long enough to breathe the air at this elevation without the aid of her suit, its compressor currently humming lightly at her spine.

She could never quite fathom that while her unsuited frame weighed fifty-nine kg on Earth, here, she weighed less than two. Here, a mere handful of drone-like hoverblades attached to her envirosuit could move her through the air with ease.

Restful. Peaceful. A far better way to start her day than the coffee she'd once guzzled as a Chicago homicide detective.

A light buzz at her wrist from the AI bracelet, which had automatically connected to her suit systems. 'Liane,' Alice, her AI, spoke inside her helmet softly, 'Asim Qadir at Environmental asks if you could take a lower pass while you're out. His greencams got knocked offline last night.'

Liane stifled a sigh. Her early morning flights were the only time she took for herself. And she knew she was about to have a really unpleasant day. Kicking someone off a colony was never a pleasure. Being in the middle of your boss's domestic dispute was even worse. It only went downhill when your boss was Benjamin Martin Donovan, Sr.—billionaire, inventor, philanthropist, and the brain behind the Sensorium and half the rest of the innovations that made modern life possible.

'Alice, please tell Asim I never pass up a chance to get a peek at tiger cubs, but aren't we supposed to be letting the wildlife in the preserve develop without seeing humans?' She glanced up at the dome, seeing the dark lines that criss-crossed its inner surfaces, the regular pattern of darker lines that were the tramways and ropelines that connected the wide-spread bubble-like human habitations which floated so lightly above the crater below.

A buzz, and then Asim's light accent resounded in her ear. 'All my cameras are down, Chief,' he told Liane tightly. 'Could be poachers. Though how they think they'd get an animal or its parts back out through the docking station, I have no idea.'

'I'll take a look around,' Liane promised, and dropped into a pike position to begin her slow dive towards the trees below. Then, she spread out wide, kicking the fan blades back on as she began to descend past the first branches, making her way effortlessly, quadrant by quadrant, through the dim, green world.

A light on her right arm swept the branches as she noted lammergeiers circling ahead of her—the bearded vultures largely ate the bones of dead prey, but she knew they weren't above snatching morsels of flesh away from the large predators that stalked the forest below—the Siberian tigers, the brown bears. There was a whole savannah biome on the western side of the dome, where lions roamed and polar bears gambolled across a frozen sea where drills had found one of Vesta's pockets of internal ice and triggered an outflow.

All courtesy of Benjamin Donovan's vision.

Closer now, and more careful—the lammergeiers might strike at her mid-air for threatening their food. They and the other birds had adapted to the low gravity and thin air with remarkable rapidity. The tigers hadn't been far behind—they'd been seen climbing the sequoias, leaping branch to branch with slow-motion feline ease. As if they'd been born to glide slowly through the air, giving a sinuous twist as their paws encountered a trunk, and then deflecting into the foliage again like ghosts.

Liane gave the branches around her a quick glance as atavistic fear trickled down her spine. The tigers could be anywhere, and being off the ground was no guarantee of safety.

And then she spotted something on the forest floor. An adult male tiger, tearing at the body of what seemed to be some prey animal. But the body seemed too small to be one of the many species of deer that roamed the forest.

With a shock, Liane recognised something she hadn't seen since leaving her job as a homicide detective five years earlier: the crumpled form of a dead human body. Suitless, at that, which suggested that whoever it was had to have *hiked* here through the prohibited-entry lower biomes. Possibly without a breather. *Maybe hypoxia set in, bad judgement . . . who knows?* 'Alice, activate my shockers. I don't want to hurt the tiger, but I need to get it away. We need to be able to identify who our poacher or tourist is.'

Shock drones emerged from compartments tucked along Liane's back and drifted towards the tiger, emitting a threatening hum that made the beast snarl and back away suspiciously. No radio collar on this one—it had been born here, among the leaf litter and thin layer of topsoil that separated the man-made biome from the underlying regolith through which the sequoias' roots struggled.

As Liane hovered above, taking pictures for the record, she sucked in a breath. The face was torn and bloodied, but . . . *oh, god damn it. It's Benjamin. How the hell is he out here—why— he wouldn't come out here on his own—if he's dead, why hasn't all hell broken loose with alerts—*

And just then, all hell *did* break loose, as one of her two deputies called in. 'Chief?' Isaiah Oluwusi said in her ear. 'We've got a big problem. The security protocols on Mr Donovan's habitat are reporting that his heartbeat failed, ma'am, but he's not inside—'

'Yeah,' Liane muttered, still staring down at the body in shock. *The alerts from his habitat AI only just* now *went off?* 'I just tripped over him. Get Asim on the line. I'm going to need to borrow some people from Environmental to cordon off the area, start an investigation, and retrieve the body. And call in Dr Hernandez. She needs to put on her medical examiner hat, because I don't think this is what you'd call natural causes.' A pause. 'Lock down the docking station and shut down the outer ring tram. No one leaves till I give the word.'

Oluwusi exhaled. 'We're getting a load of tourists and contractors in,' he warned. 'They're not going to like that.'

'It's on my authority as the chief law enforcement officer,' Liane growled into the microphone. *Okay. One of only three law enforcement officers here.* 'They can hate it all they want. The guy who built this place is dead, and someone here is responsible.' *Current domestic dispute, usually the first person to look at would be his girlfriend.*

'Ah . . . Chief?' Oluwusi's voice sounded tight.

She sighed. 'Yes?'

'Mr Donovan's son is on the inbound tram, heading to the docking area from the spaceport.'

Liane blinked. Then swore. 'God damn it, why was *that* not included on my calendar?'

'Mr Donovan told me not to tell you.' Oluwusi sounded uncomfortable. 'Said he wanted to introduce you to his son himself.'

She looked up at the interlacing green branches overhead, the darker latticework of the dome high above, and the heavens beyond. *God damn it, Benjamin. Which of the billions of people you pissed off finally got to you, here in your refuge? And how does your son factor into all this?*

Chapter Two

Benjamin Martin Donovan, Jr had never been to his estranged father's private enclave in the asteroid belt before. He had, in fact, never left Earth till earlier this year, when he'd received a communique from the old man—the first he'd heard from his father since his mother's death. *Come see me on Vesta. You've already removed your Sensorium wiring, so you're welcome here.*

No further communication. Not even when Martin had sent replies asking how or when to travel there. Just the monolithic silence he'd come to expect from his father.

Martin was not, generally, a man who obeyed orders, other than from the directors who'd overseen his multimillion-credit Sensorium productions over the years. He'd starred in two dozen blockbusters since his teens. Mostly of the action variety, meaning he'd stood in simulated explosions so that Wired people could *feel* the shockwaves ripple across their flesh, their nerves firing in response to the signals sent by the chip architecture embedded in their brains—the Sensorium technology that his father had engineered and sold across Earth. The technology that Donovan, Sr. had promoted as a way to let everyone regulate their minds through experiential feedback: "Live your own adventure! Get your adrenaline levels up through simulated struggle, and then regulate your serotonin levels through the feel of a human hand touching your own. No drugs required!"

And then, inexplicably, his father had abandoned the technology. Sold off forty-nine per cent of his holdings in Virtual Sensorium, Inc. and plunged all his resources into building a wildlife refuge as far from the rest of humanity as possible. Only people who had no Sensorium Wiring, or who'd had theirs surgically removed, were allowed into the preserve. Which, as a wholly-owned private colony, made and enforced its own rules and regulations.

Rules and regulations that had kept Martin from visiting his father for fifteen years. Not that he'd been invited. Not that he'd *wanted* to visit what seemed more like the grave of a relationship than a living one.

When Martin had been interviewed by reporters about his father, he had learned to put on his most disarming smile and say, 'It's always been challenging to be the son of one of the most brilliant men on Earth. Now that we have to say "in the solar system", it hasn't gotten easier. But I think we're good.'

A little light humour to deflect the reporters from the subsequent lie usually worked like a charm.

In truth, Benjamin Martin Donovan, Sr. was, in his son's opinion, an absolute asshole. His mind had always been so locked on the Big Ideas that he'd seemed more distant than the moon to his son. In public, Donovan had been almost affectless, his face going slack and still for sometimes as much as half a minute when asked a question by a reporter that required an answer to be procured from somewhere deep in the recesses of his mind. Martin couldn't count the number of times when, as a boy, he'd seen his mother, Clara, laugh and interpose a return question for the reporter, while his father cogitated on what Great Answer he would eventually speak.

And yet, I craved his attention, his love, Martin thought resignedly. He'd been to enough counselling for his addictions and other problems over the years to understand the inner workings of his own mind.

Though understanding never seemed to give him any more control over it.

He'd landed at the tiny spaceport, largely established for the mining consortiums that sent drone fleets out into the asteroid belt from Vesta and Ceres, with the occasional human flight team for larger jobs. Boarded a tram with a surprising number of bearded miners and workers, along with a handful of wealthy tourists. His father kept the dome as billionaires of the past had kept private islands, partially subsidising it as a retreat for those wealthy enough to venture there for the thrill of 'roughing it' in the asteroid belt—though without actually experiencing much in the way of privation or primitive living. At ten thousand hydrogen credits a night, plus the cost of the space trip to Vesta, it remained something out of reach for all but the wealthiest of Earth's population.

But those wealthy tourists were easily identifiable by their fresh, unmarked spacesuits and the way they watched the tram's walls and ceilings, as if they could collapse at any moment. The workers, however, just secured their helmets, settled their heads back on the seats, and dozed off.

Humans are funny. We can get used to just about anything, Martin thought, his head spinning with exhaustion. He hadn't slept the night before. Second- and third-guessing the decision that had led him here, all over again. He'd headed to the ship's gym to work out some of the stress—he'd all but lived in the gym for the past year of the trip. *I want returning to Earth's gravity to be an* option *once I'm done with whatever amends I can* actually *make with the old man.*

Deciding to take his mind off the issues, Martin nudged the worker beside him on the seat before the man fell completely asleep. 'Hey—mind telling me about your job here on Vesta?' he asked in his friendliest fashion.

The man raised his faceshield, revealing angular features and a dark goatee, trimmed neatly to avoid conflicting with breathing gear. 'Huh. You look familiar. You a reporter?'

'Nah. I'm only nosy on a freelance basis.' Martin extended a hand. 'Call me Marty.'

The man chuckled. 'Hey, Marty. I'm Claude Bensoussan. And I don't mind talking. See, Mr Donovan brings in contractors and specialists for work on the habitat.' His eyes shifted to the side momentarily. 'My company's got me here to handle repairs on some of the robotic crawlers that chew up the regolith and turn it into atmosphere. We're supposed to be shipping some more folks here in the next few months, but there's some snafu in the payment department.' He shrugged. 'I'm sure it'll get straightened out. Guys like Mr Donovan just throw money around till the problem's solved.'

Martin ignored that. 'Are you all a team?' he asked, gesturing at the rest of the workers.

A snort. 'Nah. Half these guys are from other corporations here on Vesta. Asteroid miners, drone jockeys.' He hesitated. 'They were saying that they're here for a personal meeting with Mr Donovan. Something about worker conditions on the rock.' The man shrugged. 'Don't know what good it'll do them to talk to the man. Not like he cuts their cheques.'

'Probably not much,' Martin agreed amiably, his interest in the conversation waning.

The man leaned back, closing his eyes again as the tram jostled lightly over the tracks. 'Ever wonder what it's like being one of them?' he asked sleepily.

'Eh?' Martin replied, having gone back to staring at the screen that showed the ragged terrain over which they sped in lieu of a window. The bright diamonds that spread across the sky like a necklace of light—the satellites that condensed the sun's rays for the use of the colonies on and under the surface. He'd already moved on to wondering other things, such as, if the asteroid completed one full rotation every five hours (dizzying, compared to Earth's sedate twenty-four hour revolution), would he be able to see the stars swirling around the foreshortened horizon? Did they have to cycle the satellites between bright and dim to simulate day and night for the animals and plants in his father's preserve? 'One of them,' he repeated, buying himself time to find a socially-acceptable response. 'The rich and shameless, you mean?'

A smile cracked the man's face. 'Yeah. Life at the top, anything you want, you just have to snap your fingers. Like Donovan's son. The actor. Groupies, parties, drugs.'

Does he recognise me? No. Doesn't seem to be in my face. And it doesn't sound like a passive-aggressive attempt to get me to react. 'I try not to think about crap like that,' Martin managed, putting just the right amount of down-to-earth finality in his voice. 'Doesn't do me any good.'

'Yeah, you're probably right.' The man sealed his faceshield and appeared to go to sleep.

Martin grimaced and turned back to the screen. He'd shaved his hair down to a buzzcut on the ship that had brought him here, and grown his beard out to keep his famous features a little more unrecognisable. So far, no one on the tram had done more than give him a dubious squint.

It never ceased to amaze him. The fans who thought they *knew* him, who'd temporarily lived in his body through the power of the Sensorium—or, god help him, the ones who'd gotten hold of the *sex tape* one of his exes had made without his consent, who thought they knew every inch of his body— could be sitting beside him right now, and they probably wouldn't recognise him when he hadn't turned on what he thought of as his 'performing charm'. *Well, you never have to turn it back on again. You made enough money in the business that you don't need to work another day if you don't want to. Not a credit of it from dear old Dad, either.*

Taking out the Sensorium chips had meant *retirement*, his agent had warned. The only acting gigs that would remain would be old-fashioned 2D movies for the retro crowd, or live stage performances like a Broadway run. Neither interested Martin. He was as done with that chapter of his life as . . . *as my father was done with Earth. Huh. Guess we're more alike than I thought.*

At that moment, the tram crested a final ridge, and Martin's eyes widened as he caught sight of the Rheasilvia preserve for the first time. 'Holy shit,' he muttered, astounded despite himself.

The screen image couldn't capture the whole scale, of course. And 'dome' was a misleading word, as sheets of gleaming Demron, a metal-impregnated polyethylene, sleeked down from Amalthea's peak to the rim of the crater, supported by graphene struts and buoyed by the pressure of the atmosphere within. It looked like a cross between a silver egg and the universe's largest pyramid. *You never do anything by halves, do you, Dad?* Martin thought silently, awe mingling with grim humour. *Besides dealing with people, that is. God damn.* 'What do they do if they get an asteroid impact? Won't that pop the dome?' he muttered out loud.

'It's thicker than it looks,' a man in the seat behind him replied, startling Martin. 'And there are fleets of microbots you can't see from here, constantly crawling around, looking for damage, and repairing it. And each cross-section of the arches has an independent failsafe system. Throws a patch across if there's ever a breach. Still pays to keep your suit on inside, as far as I'm concerned. And not just 'cause the air's thin.' He shrugged. 'Rumour mill has it that Donovan's planning on freighting in materials from other asteroids and just tenting the whole of Vesta. I mean, it'd take centuries, but . . . pharaohs gotta have pyramids, I guess.'

Martin swallowed. *Why do you want me to see this, Dad?* he wondered. *It's not like you've ever needed my approval. So why now?*

The tram came to a halt at its dock, where an airlock complex would let them enter once they'd passed a security checkpoint. Except . . . the two security people stationed at the debarkation zone wouldn't let anyone pass.

'What's the meaning of this?' demanded a petulant woman in a skin-tight, elasticised suit. In spite of the rigours of space travel, Martin noticed that she'd still applied foundation, mascara, the works. 'I have a reservation—a very *expensive* reservation. I want to speak with your manager!'

Martin noted the guards' shifting eyes and tight-lipped demeanours. 'I'm sorry, ma'am. Station's locked down. Security chief's orders. There's been an incident.'

'What *sort* of incident?' the woman demanded stridently.

Martin removed his helmet, debating walking to the front of the line and asking what the holdup was. Putting the family name and his famous face to work in his favour for once.

And that's when a small, tough-looking woman exited the airlock behind the guards, bounce-stepping directly towards Martin with a flowing ease that suggested she'd spent a lot of time on this airless rock. 'Mr Donovan,' she murmured when she reached him, not looking directly at him. A sidelong glance that seemed to take in many things at once. 'Liane Sheridan, station security. I'm sorry to meet you under these circumstances.'

There was nothing good that could follow a sentence like that. 'What circumstances are these?' Martin asked, matching her soft tone, even as he noted his fellow passengers pulling back around them, creating a bubble of space filled mostly with whispers. *Damn it. They heard the name.*

'If you come with me, I can explain,' the security officer replied. Her eyes held shadows.

'Am I going to need to call my lawyer?' Martin asked mildly—a reflex from his wilder days. He didn't turn on the charm of his mobile smile and features. Something in the shadows of her eyes forbade it.

'Your lawyer's going to have an eighty-minute time delay to get back to you once you call, and then another eighty minutes for their reply to get back to you.' She finally made eye contact, the corners of her mouth turning down. 'Chances are, you're going to be talking to a few, yeah. But I'm not *taking you in*, as it were.' A wave at the dome. 'Not that we even have a brig. Come along, Mr Donovan.'

In the airlock, listening to it hum, Martin braced himself against the metal of the hatch and said, 'Chief Sheridan, I think you can call me Martin. My father is Mr Donovan, as far as I'm concerned.' His throat tightened. 'Has something happened to him?'

'Why do you ask, Mr Donovan?' Immediate shift into a questioning mode, he noticed. Refusing the offer of more familiarity, declining to give a reply.

'Because if life were a script, there's only one thing that would come after a "sorry to meet you this way, please step aside where no one can hear us" opening line.' Martin sighed. 'He's had heart problems for years. Ironic, considering the fact that I never thought he *had* a heart, growing up. Is he in the clinic?' He didn't want to say anything more fatal, as if saying the words out loud would make them more real.

She started to reach out a hand to put it on his shoulder, but pulled back as if he emitted some kind of toxic radiation. 'I . . . no.' She exhaled as the airlock clicked open, allowing them entrance to the vast dome beyond. 'There's no easy way to say this. But your father is dead, and the circumstances are highly suspicious.'

Each bouncing step as he followed her out should have made him feel as carefree as a child, although inside . . . nothing but cold and lead. 'Suspicious how?' Martin asked, his tone vacant as he probed for some kind of emotional reaction inside of himself.

'I found his body out in the forest preserve, where no one's permitted on foot. Time of death was several hours before that, but the sensors embedded in his pacemaker didn't alert his house AI that he'd died until just past six am Zulu.' Crisp, brisk words as she gestured towards a lift that ran along one of the graphene struts.

He grabbed one of the loops of rope inside the platform, just as she did, and watched in mild consternation as the clear walls enclosed them and they moved upwards.

She continued, 'Our resident doctor is undertaking an autopsy, but it may take her some time to find a cause of death.'

'Why so?' Martin asked, trying to sound nonchalant while holding on for dear life as the lift reached the point where the struts and canopy changed from vertical to a steep incline, and began rushing inwards towards the huge mountain at the centre of the crater. 'Good *god*,' he muttered reflexively, his hands starting to sweat. 'How high up *are* we?'

'Only four km so far.' He couldn't tell if amusement lurked under her clinical tone. 'The peak is twenty-two point five km from the crater's depths. Thirteen miles. Terminal velocity here is currently about fourteen miles per hour, not the hundred and forty it is on Earth. In a fall here, you generally have time to increase your drag coefficient by spreading out, and then bend your knees for the landing. A bad fall will still break bones, yeah. But it's not certain death here, unlike on Earth.'

'Just *uncertain* death. How comforting.'

Her voice had been so calm, so casual, that it came as a shock when she flipped to a more biting, acerbic tone now. 'I find it very interesting, Mr Donovan, that you're exhibiting more of a reaction to heights than to your father's death.'

Martin wrapped both hands around the rope. 'Chief, I fully expect to have to have long and expensive conversations with my therapist about the latest of my *daddy-abandonment* issues.' Self-deprecating irony laced his tone. 'But at this exact moment, in and around being abjectly terrified for my life—' the lift continued to move upwards in a graceful arc, and as far as he could tell, the damned thing was still accelerating, '—most of what I feel is a mix of irritation and a strong sense of… *of course. Of course*, after fifteen years of silence, he calls me out here, and *of course* before we can have whatever deeply awkward and uncomfortable interaction he planned to inflict on us both, he dies.' Martin turned his head and gave her a tight, controlled smile, lifting his eyebrows. 'Ms Sheridan? This is *par for the fucking course* in terms of my relationship with the old man.'

Her lips lifted into a reluctant smile, and somehow, Martin breathed a little easier. 'Am I a suspect in your investigation?' he managed as they finally levelled out and the lift slowed down, heading towards what looked like a docking platform. Criss-crossing graphene beams, which looked like little more than solidified smoke, ran between the wide, arcing struts that rose up from the ground towards Amalthea's peak, making diamond patterns.

Attached to this latticework were silvery bubbles, which bobbed gently in the air currents, or from movement inside. After a moment, Martin remembered the video guide he'd watched on his flight in. 'Those are the *houses*?' he muttered. 'How does anyone ever go to sleep around here? One of those gets knocked loose, and you just . . . fall.'

'We've got nets below the houses and the tramways,' Sheridan replied, shrugging. 'A lot of birds like to use the nets as perches. Look down—careful,' she added, putting an arm out across his chest as he bent. Swayed. Edged back from the door of the lift. 'You get used to it,' she added, her tone more kindly than it had been. 'You also get used to fact that everything moves like you're in a bouncy castle.'

She handed him a belt attached to a cable with a carabiner at one end and locking it onto her own belt. 'Can't go losing the boss's son. Put this on. I'll pull you along, if you need it. Keep in mind that the atmosphere is really thin at our current height— about as thin as at the top of the Andes. You've been trucking along on a ship set to the atmospheric pressure of sea level on Earth for the better part of a year. You may feel lightheaded.'

'Why not just build habitats at ground level?' Martin demanded. 'Or tunnel into the mountain? Was that just too sane and rational for my father?'

Sheridan paused, flashing him a brief smile. 'The structural stability of tunnels in the mountain is a little uncertain. There's a lot of ice and regolith, and not a lot of gravity. So, tunnels are a "next step", but it'll require a lot of impact studies. The crater floor is for the plants and animals,' she explained. 'We're supposed to live above them as caretakers. That's half of what my job is—keeping people from going down and messing with the new biomes. He had some ideas about carrying capacity and low-impact living, and the bubble habitats were his way of trying to test the ideas out. I—ah… From going through what's left of his file systems this morning, I know he left some recordings for you. Maybe he explains it better there.'

What's left *of his file systems,* Martin picked out of the rapid-fire sequence of words. 'What do you mean—ah, hell—' His words cut off as she simply started pulling herself along a series of ropes that hung parallel to the ground, so far below, swinging underneath them like a monkey. Martin, attached to her, had little option but to follow . . . swinging behind her like the monkey's tail.

'This doesn't feel safe,' he shouted as he arced up and got a hand on the line beside her, his heart hammering in his chest.

'It's fine. I just need to get you to where we store suits with hoverblade attachments,' she called back. 'Mostly, when we travel between habitats, it's people power—it's really important to get what exercise you can here, before you turn into an amoeba. But for new folks, and if you head out of the living zone, there are hoverblades.'

Halfway across this odd highway in the sky, Martin realised something. 'You didn't answer my question,' he called. 'Am I a suspect?'

Sheridan leapt lightly up onto a platform and reached out a hand, easily hauling him up beside her. 'We usually look at close family first,' she replied, looking down and away. 'That's where we started fifteen years ago. When your mother died.'

Martin froze. 'You . . . worked my mom's case.'

'Yeah. I was a rookie.' She shot a quick, sidelong glance up at him. 'You were in rehab.'

I couldn't even make it out of the clinic to go to the funeral. All that hearing of her death did was send me all the way back down to the bottom of the pit I'd dug for myself. Martin swallowed. 'And now you're working for my dad.' It wasn't a question.

'He'd kept track of me. I stood out.' She made a face. 'I'm allergic, broadly speaking, to the Sensorium implants. Can't have 'em. He also said he liked how I asked questions. So, when he started building this place, and we were exchanging letters, he asked me to come along.' She looked away again, expressionless. 'I'd seen enough murder for a lifetime, so I said yes. Didn't think it'd follow me here so soon.'

Martin felt as if all the air had been let out of him. Thinking about his mother's death tended to have that effect. *I wasn't there. I was across the country. Useless waste of space that I am— no.* Stop that. 'So, what motive do you think I'd have?' he asked, his voice lifeless. 'I've long since been out of his will.'

'What few of his records haven't been scrambled, show that he'd called his lawyers to put you back in,' she replied, ushering him inside one of the silvery habitation bubbles. Inside, the plain austerity of an office. Three touchscreen desks. The smell of human skin.

'So, someone *did* scramble his files.'

'Yeah. I've got my AI trying to reconstruct things, but it's a mess.' She blew a strand of hair out of her eyes, her expression taut. 'Probably trying to conceal any video taken of the crime itself by his house security system. And probably to conceal whatever the motive was. House entry and exit logs are gone for the past week. And I've got a suspect list that ranges from his only living family—' an oddly apologetic look flashed through her eyes, 'to the girlfriend he'd asked me to escort off the premises, to the other thousand people who live in the habitat, to the HaveNot faction of the Belt corporations, to the billion or so people back home who're addicted to the Sensorium. But in the end, though, there are only really a few motives for killing someone. Rage. Jealousy. Envy. Money. Power. People tend to be really predictable that way.'

Martin's mouth had fallen open. 'Wait. Whoa. Back that up a bit. Dad had a *girlfriend*?' He blinked. 'I thought he'd been doing the whole celibacy thing since, well, Mom.' He wanted to roll his eyes, but fixed them on the floor, because instead of discussing his father's foibles as an amusing anecdote—*yeah, he spent a year in a Buddhist monastery, guess the vow of silence wasn't* challenging *enough for him*—it became something final. Something *past tense.*

And while he could feel the wave of grief hovering over him, it was like a tsunami—the water had pulled far back from shore, and wouldn't hit him for a while yet. But when it came down, he had a dim sense that he was going to drown. *Losing one parent to murder was bad enough. Losing both . . . damn. This is going to hurt when the shock wears off. Who knew?*

Sheridan cleared her throat. 'Er, this one was number three, I think?' she offered. 'None of his relationships have lasted longer than eighteen months, as far as I can tell. He never gave me reasons for why there was a break-up. Just . . . "please expedite Ms Jablonksi's departure. Thank you".' She met his eyes as he brought them up from the floor, and gestured at a suit hanging nearby. 'Here. This was fabricated for you. Your father had it waiting.' She shook her head. 'Wish to god I knew why he kept your arrival a secret from me. It's not like I was going to go all fangirl.'

He regarded her, grateful for the momentary distraction. Catching just a hint of a flush along her cheeks. His lips twitched involuntarily. 'Chief, I would never accuse you of being a *fan* of mine,' Martin replied gravely, but with just a hint of teasing behind it. 'But, just theoretically, if you were, how would that work, if you're allergic to Sensorium implants?'

Sheridan sighed. '*Theoretically*,' she responded, sounding mildly harried, 'I would've had to find a theatre that had converted the Sensorium footage back to 2D film, because I'm *also* susceptible to motion sickness, so 3D doesn't work for me either. That, and your father had all of your films here in 2D.'

Martin blinked, moved by both revelations. *Dad* actually *watched my stuff?* 'That would also mean, hypothetically speaking, that you would actually have had to like my acting. Because you'd have experienced it solely from the outside. You wouldn't have been feeling what I felt against my skin, or, given the chance to play one of my co-stars, you wouldn't have, say, felt my hand gripping yours.' *Is that—yes, she's definitely blushing now.* He kept his tone neutral as he went on. 'Chief, if any of this were true, I'd have to say that it was one of the nicest things anyone has ever said to me. Because I'm fairly sure that absolutely no one has ever paid to watch me *act*.' He gave a slight snort.

Her chin lifted and she replied, 'And if so, I'd tell you that they wouldn't have converted Sensorium data to 2D for just one person, and to stop being ridiculously self-effacing, because it's totally blowing your image.' She gestured at the suit impatiently. 'There's a dressing room over there. Get changed. It'll be safer getting you to your father's house that way.'

He picked up the suit. It didn't have a hard outer shell. It wouldn't repel bullets or shrapnel. But it had an elasticised interior that he recognised. Some spacesuits used this design to maintain pressure on the body, rather than filling the entire suit with air.

He studied the rest of its features. A light helmet with a breather mask. Hoses snaking back to mysterious destinations along the spine. Long brackets along the arms, legs, and back, in which he could see hoverblades, ready to pop out when needed. It was also glossy, white, and he knew it would be skin-tight. 'Good thing I kept up the workout regimen for the year of the trip,' he managed to joke, though it fell flat in the air. 'If you all wear these, I guess there's a reason for all the exercise.'

'Your father was a big believer in exercise as a method of enhancing serotonin flow. He was deeply invested in finding a better way for humans not just to exist, but to *live*.' She turned away, and his eyes followed her momentarily. Her black suit was as close-fitting as his own, but held several additional panels along the forearms. *Storage slots*, he figured. And armour plates all along her torso that looked much shinier than the rest of her suit, which was scuffed and worn. *She doesn't usually wear the tactical gear. She's spooked as hell, but covering it well.*

Another thought occurred then. 'Is it going to be okay for me to go in there? I mean . . . is it where it—' The words suddenly stuck in his throat, and Martin sat down on the edge of a desk heavily. *Damn it. I do not want to see where he died.* 'Is it the crime scene?' He lifted his head. 'I mean, you did just say you always start with the family.' *And I'm technically a suspect.*

She turned back towards him, her smile fading. 'Well, I'd also usually start with whoever "found" the body, since quite often, the killer wants attention on some level, and makes the call that alerts us. But since *I'm* the one who found him, I'm fairly certain I can rule myself out.' Her expression suggested that it hadn't been a pretty sight. 'We've scanned the entire place, top to bottom. It's all recorded. And I want to hear any messages he left for you under voice-lock before whoever scrambled his house AI manages to delete those too.'

Martin nodded, swallowing. 'So do I.'

Chapter Three

Benjamin Donovan's Sr.'s home on the Olympian Ring, closest to the mountain, was considerably larger than Liane's own habitat, which perched above the security offices. But it was still much smaller than any opulent manor on Earth, being comprised of four spheres, each connected to each other and to the cross brace above them. A bathing and hygiene area, a kitchen, a large living space with plush carpets lining the floors, netted chairs hanging from the ceiling and, and a sleeping chamber with a comfortable bed platform, also hanging from the ceiling. Martin had given that last item a thoughtful push with one foot, watching it swing back and forth with a dubious shake of his head. 'I like a little more stability in my own furniture,' Liane had told him, and he'd given her a blinding flash of a smile in response.

Currently, Liane stood behind Benjamin Donovan Sr.'s desk, paging through search results with her fingertips, as her AI Alice continued to comb through decades of files, conducting multiple searches simultaneously. The detective kept one eye on Martin, however, where he sat in a swaying chair in the main living area of the habitat, listening to another of his father's messages.

While he was tall and in excellent shape, seeing him slumped in on himself took away from the larger-than-life qualities he possessed on screen. She'd braced herself for that, mentally. Steeled herself for seeing his father in him, instead of the carefully-controlled flickers of facial expression that were his hallmark on the movie screen. Sensorium *impression*. Whatever.

No one was ever who or what they seemed at a distance. You made up, inferred a person from the pieces of themselves they distributed through social media. But it was never the *whole* person; personhood had become performative for everyone in the past several decades, not just Hollywood types. So, everyone also became detectives by default, trying to discern reality from all these disparate pieces of information.

Still, Martin looked lost and alone, dwarfed by the dark shadows in that area of the wide, silvery, spherical room.

'What's this one about?' she called over, wanting to erase the look of blank confusion and desolation on his face.

He blinked, mobility and life returning to his face. Then he looked from the screen to her, and then at the screen again. 'I have no idea. I think I just zoned out. Let me start it over again. It's dated February 18 of last year—about a week after he contacted me to tell me "get over here".'

Onscreen, Benjamin Donovan Sr.'s face—so like his son's, but somehow lacking in all the mobile grace that characterised the younger man's features—began to drone. 'John B. Calhoun predicted our current sociological collapse as early as 1972, with his "rat paradise". Within five generations, the rats overpopulated his careful environment, and began displaying atypical behaviours. Adolescent males, even in proximity to abundant food, displayed aberrant violence. Females stopped having litters, or abandoned their young. The rats that had secluded living spaces, but had nothing better to do with their time than groom and socialise? They survived the longest, but lost the will to continue their species. They no longer had sex or produced offspring or even interacted with one another. They just drifted along, existing.'

Donovan blew out a mouthful of marijuana smoke and stared into space. After a long moment, he went on calmly, monotonously, steadily. 'We are the rats. We have abundant food, but no space away from one another on Earth. There are generations of young humans growing up without adversity, without struggle, without *meaningful work*—generations of account managers and social media specialists who make nothing, do nothing, accomplish nothing—and go home to their tiny apartments to isolate themselves further. They groom themselves carefully. The males go out and can't find mates, and seethe in frustration and anger. The females retreat to higher ground, safer areas, and delay childbearing, or don't have children at all. And everything becomes a game of social signalling, a competition of people shouting louder and louder from within their tiny, confined spaces to be heard, while simultaneously desperately trying to get away from the sound of all those other voices. That's why, in my opinion, social media *created* more neuroses than it helped to solve. It created an echo chamber of voices from which people couldn't escape, even in the privacy of their own homes. It made every space feel overwhelmingly overpopulated. Overstimulating. Exhausting.'

Another inhale of smoke. An exhalation. 'The Sensorium was supposed to change that. It was supposed to give people a solid whack to the cerebellum. The sensation of physical contact, to ramp up the serotonin in the brain. So that they wouldn't feel alone or isolated, but stabilised within a perfect pocket of *just enough*. So that the carrying capacity of the land, carrying capacity of the heart, could be amplified. Extended.' He sighed. 'All I did was create a new addiction. Which is why, after your mother's death, I had all of my own wiring removed. I'd become as much an addict as anyone else. And I couldn't enable people anymore. I sold off forty-nine per cent of Virtual Sensorium. Enough to retain control. To try to wind the damn thing down. But once you've let the genie out of the bottle . . . it's damned hard to push it back in. Try to grab a handful of smoke.' Onscreen, he did just that to the white veils rising from his joint. 'Useless. Pitiful effort.'

Martin paused the playback. 'I'd like to point out that when *he* smokes a joint, it's perfectly fine. If *I* light up, it's addiction.' He rubbed at his eyes. 'Why the hell come all the way out here, Dad?' he muttered. 'What's living like a hermit got to do with your sociological maundering?'

Liane shrugged. 'He talked about it now and again. He wanted to create a "rat paradise" for humans, but better. With adequate living space, population controls that worked, and everyone in the environment having meaningful work and ample opportunities to pursue art and recreation. The stuff that Calhoun said seemed to help the rats. Except . . . the rats that had, effectively, brain damage and social damage from years of living in the crowded circumstances? They never got better. It had to be done for the *next* generation, which recovered when they were raised under those circumstances.' She sighed. 'Maybe he wanted to prove it out here, and then try to incorporate it into the next-gen Sensorium?' She gestured at the screen. 'He might get into it further on.'

'There's *hours* of it here. Maybe he was dictating it all as a diary, and that's why it was never sent. 'Cause he hasn't complained yet about my lack of replies.' Martin's fingers slid over the screen, displaying the hundreds of recorded messages left by his father for him. 'He was averaging close to two of these a week,' he noted. 'Damn it.'

He looked exhausted. Liane restrained the urge to pat him on the shoulder. People probably thought they had the *right* to touch him because he was a Sensorium star, but she figured he needed his space. 'Maybe skip to the end. See if he was good enough to record any suspicious activities by people near and dear to him,' Liane suggested, folding her arms over her chest.

As he reached for the controls again, Alice chimed softly in her ear. 'You've got results for me?' Liane asked.

'Medical examiner report is in.'

'Link up to the screen. I'd like Mr Donovan to be able to hear you.'

Alice appeared on the big screen, sliding across to divide the space with the message console. She looked like a cartoon character, a blonde child with a blue pinafore dress and black saddle shoes, carrying, for the moment, a teacup far too large for her hands.

'*Through the Looking Glass?*' Martin asked, giving Liane a slightly disbelieving glance.

Liane gestured at one of the windows, which looked out on the crater below. 'I live in Wonderland, don't I? Okay, Alice. Tell me what Dr Hernandez has found so far.'

Alice nodded, replying pleasantly, 'Time of death set at one am Zulu. Six hours before you found the body.'

'Which means that his house systems didn't register his death for six hours.'

'Obviously.' Alice reproved in her British accent.

Liane let that one pass. 'What was the cause of death?'

'Massive overdose of insulin to a non-diabetic individual, administered through an injection. Dr Hernandez suggests that he likely fell into a coma rapidly.'

Liane caught Martin's wince and gently put in, 'It's likely that he felt nauseous and tired and simply fell asleep, Mr Donovan. There would've been little pain.'

'Yes,' Alice agreed. 'But all of this made it imperative to dump the body where the animals could get at it quickly to erase the evidence.'

'We have any insulin-dependent diabetics on the station?' Liane asked.

'Fourteen out of a thousand permanent residents. Dr Hernandez said that you would ask. She also notes that there have been guests who have brought their supplies with them in the past, but there haven't been diabetic visitors in the past three years. It's considered too dangerous to travel so far from where medical supply chains can easily reach.'

Liane flicked her fingers in acknowledgement. 'Do we have names on the permanent residents who require insulin?' Her mind spun in controlled patterns. *How likely is it that a diabetic would use their own supply, put their own lives at risk to kill someone else?* 'Have any of them reported thefts?' *And we'll have to look at their associates, too. . .*

'Alan Smith. Dr Asim Qadir. Rahul Basak. Vardah Parsamyan. Delores Chatterjee. Teresa Chuquisengo.' The litany went on for quite some time before Alice concluded, 'None have reported thefts yet.'

'Great. Teresa is one of my deputies. Which could explain why security systems seem to have gone completely down.'

Liane hated thinking this way, but she had to. Sticking her head in the sand wouldn't accomplish anything. 'Of course, Vardah is chief of system operations and, oh, look, Rahul is in ground operations for the ecology team, with access to the greencams. Couldn't be easy.' Liane sighed as she flicked through the list of names and occupations. 'What are your diagnostics for the house systems showing so far?'

'I've definitely found traces of tampering in the security systems, suppressing the medical monitoring processes and routines, but whoever did it used Mr Donovan's passwords. All video of the past twenty-four hours remains scrubbed. I'm attempting reconstruction, but it will take time, depending on the thoroughness of the erasures.'

'Anything else?'

Alice hesitated. The blue eyes onscreen seemed to shift towards Martin's frame on the netted chair.

'Just say it,' Martin told the AI tiredly. 'Whatever it is, how can it be worse than anything else I've heard today?'

'As part of routine investigation of family members, I have looked through your most recent banking transactions, Mr Donovan,' Alice replied softly.

His head rose. 'Don't you need a *warrant* for that sort of thing?'

'This is a privately-held colony. There is no actual law here, only the guidelines of the colony charter as set forth by your father,' she responded primly. 'And your bank is a subsidiary of one of your father's corporations, so I possess a certain amount of access—'

Martin turned from the AI to glare at Liane. 'I don't appreciate the breach of privacy,' he bit out. Then he exhaled. 'Alright. There shouldn't have been much activity. I bought a ticket to come here. My agent's been doing repairs on my house in preparation for probably selling it. . . figured I'd downsize and move to Colorado, assuming I could transition back to Earth gravity when I got home.' He paused. 'So, come on, what's the deal?'

Alice made a sound like a gentle cough. 'There was a large sum transferred from your accounts to that of one Claude Bensoussan this morning.'

Liane watched Martin's face. He blinked repeatedly, and then his eyes lit up with recognition. 'Claude—that's the guy I was talking to on the tram here from the spaceport. Said he was a contractor. You're saying he *hacked* me?'

Alice hesitated. Liane cleared her throat. 'Claude Bensoussan is a spokesman for the HaveNots. They're an outspoken group of miners who are trying to unionise here in the asteroid belt. He had a meeting on Mr Donovan's schedule today.'

'He said he was just a contractor.' Martin shook his head. 'Usually, I'm better at pegging liars. He made a couple of comments about spoiled rich kids, but I didn't think he even recognised me.' He looked down dourly at the banking readouts on his wrist. 'Guess I need to upgrade my security.'

Alice made a slight dinging sound. 'The payment was made in your name before you got on the tram, Mr Donovan. He would have needed to compromise your security without proximity. Or you would have needed to have made the payment before your ostensible first meeting.'

'Ostensible?' Martin grated out. 'What the *hell*?'

Liane flicked her fingers at the screen, and Alice disappeared.

Martin's face was set. 'You think these HaveNots have something to do with my dad's death? That I *paid them off* to do it?' He snorted, standing—and nearly bounced up to the ceiling, which took away from the drama of his motion. 'I give your AI full clearance to go through my message queue.' Martin slowly managed to unfold himself back to the floor, holding onto the chair's ropes to do so. 'You just *try* to find messages between me and this Claude guy—'

Liane made a face. 'I believe you.'

That halted him mid-sentence. Martin frowned. 'You do?'

'Yeah.'

'Why? Shouldn't you be tracking this down? Following every lead?'

'It's a stupid lead.' She shrugged. 'Sometimes, you have to trust your intuition in police work. And while, yes, I absolutely will go talk to Mr Bensoussan and ask about this unexpectedly large donation of—' she glanced at her wrist, eyebrows raising, 'Ten thousand hydrogen credits, my, my—'

'Fuck me!' Martin exploded. 'That's half my trip here!'

'Your father could have bought and sold you, but I don't think you're particularly going to miss the funds, Mr Donovan—'

'If you're going to insult me, you really *should* just call me Martin—'

'—the point remains that it's a *stupid* lead, that someone clearly *wants* me to follow. Probably the same person who cleared out the video in the house, the greencams in the forest, and the files in your father's servers. Clearing out everything so that all we can see is this neon arrow pointing towards you.' She rolled her eyes. 'Crimes are usually *messy*. This is all nice and neat and has a bow on it, except for the fact that neither you nor Bensoussan has a history that suggests that you have extensive computer capabilities.'

'How do you know anything about him?'

She lifted her wrist, where Alice was flashing information on Claude Bensoussan. Minor arrests twenty years ago for civil disorder in Morocco. Employment in robotics, yes, programming skills with regard to command-and-control modules onboard such devices, but no signs of security breach training. *Though how much security breach expertise do you need when you have the victim's passwords? Though that again begs the question of* how *someone obtained the passwords . . .*

Liane exhaled. Reached up and gingerly put a hand on his shoulder. Human to human. 'I should be looking at people on my own team for security breach knowledge. Maybe Asim's folks, since they handle the greencams.' She paused. 'Did Claude say anything else to you on the tram?'

She could feel his shrug ripple through him. 'Just that his firm hadn't been paid for recent work with the robots here. Sounded legitimately annoyed about that.'

Something clicked at the back of Liane's head. 'Unpaid contracts? Huh. Alice? Could you add that to your search parameters? Unpaid contracts here in the habitat in the last, oh, eighteen months to two years?'

'On it!' Alice chirped from her wrist as Liane started to move away, her hand slipping from Martin's shoulder.

He caught it, though. Held it lightly, loosely. 'Thank you for believing me,' Martin told her simply. 'It's an unusual experience for me. Most of the time, people look at the record from the parties-and-drugs days, and think that's . . . all I am. All I'll ever be.' A quick, rueful grin. 'It's the first thing I figure most people think when they look at me. That or, you know, the whole sex tape thing.' He released her fingers and shifted away.

Odd to see an expression of acute vulnerability on his face. Though of course, he could also be playing on her sympathies. She had to set her biases and sympathies aside to acknowledge that fact. But her gut reaction kept insisting, *He's for real.*

Liane was saved from having to come up with a reply as the airlock door to the habitat—so necessary, since every habitat was its own failsafe in case the dome was damaged and the atmosphere escaped—cycled open, and Erica Jablonski, a tall woman with frosted blonde hair, entered the main living area, looking surprised to find them both here. 'Chief Sheridan!' she declared, putting her hands on her hips. 'I demand to know why the tram to the spaceport is unavailable. Ben told me I was leaving today. I certainly don't intend to stay one minute more where I'm no longer wanted.'

Liane noted the up-thrust chin, the squared shoulders, the redness around the eyes that mascara and makeup couldn't hide. 'Where *is* he?' Erica demanded, her voice becoming a little higher. 'If he's going to block the exits, he should damn well be here to give me an explanation—' Her voice petered out as she took in Martin's face as he turned. 'Oh,' Erica went on. 'Well, look at you. You must be Ben's son. It's so nice to meet you?' she offered, coming towards them, extending one beringed hand. A flirtatious smile strained over other, more hidden emotions. 'Why, you look just like him. Though I *do* like the beard. Rugged. Mysterious.'

'You're better than I am,' Liane noted calmly. 'It took me a few minutes to pick him out of the crowd at the tram dock. And I've seen every film Martin's ever made.' *You don't sound surprised that he's here. Did Benjamin tell you he was coming?*

Martin's eyes flicked towards her, a quick, incisive glance that took in her sudden acquiescence on the matter of his name. The sudden suggestion of familiarity between them. '*Every* one of them?' he asked, putting on a smile that suggested Liane was the only woman in the room, while simultaneously stepping closer to stand beside her, aligned, so that their shoulders touched. As if they'd practised this before. 'I truly hope not *all* of them.'

Erica's eyes flickered between them. 'So, where's Ben, and why can't I *leave*?'

'I don't suppose you could tell me where you were between midnight and six Zulu this morning?' Liane asked mildly.

'*Packing*. Vardah was helping me.'

'Vardah Parsamyan? Chief operational officer and budgetary manager?' That last, for Martin's sake, so he could follow along more easily. 'I wasn't aware the two of you were so well acquainted that she'd help you pack. All night.' Liane put on a smile to conceal the razors in her words. She'd never liked Erica. While Benjamin Donovan had certainly lacked warmth and had been awkwardly prone to talk in word-bursts that had poured over her, she'd always felt her boss was sincere. Erica, on the other hand, was a socialite. On the board of directors for half a dozen charities, directing the flow of money she'd never earned from this source or that. *Must be nice.*

'Oh, well, yes. We've become good friends this last year. I wouldn't think who I have dinner with on a regular basis would be any of your concern. As Security Chief.' The underlining on the last phrase couldn't have been more pointed or poisonous.

Putting me in my place, eh? 'Around here, that doesn't usually amount to more than taking out the trash,' Liane agreed politely. She left that hanging there for a moment, then added, 'Speaking of which, I apologise for not having been on time to escort you to the tram. But there's been a murder, which takes priority.'

Erica had started to bristle over the implicit insult. But now, her eyes widened until the whites showed. 'Murder?' she whispered. 'Here? Who?'

'Benjamin Donovan, Sr.,' Liane replied.

Right on cue, Erica began to wail. 'No! No! Not Ben! We had our differences, but not . . . not like this. . . ' She reached out a hand, as if expecting to be caught and helped to a chair.

Martin looked at Liane over Erica's head, his expression one of distinct cynicism. His eyes flicked to the weeping woman, conveying a silent message that she could read as clearly as any in his movies: *You want me to deal with this?*

Liane nodded, trying to express regret with a shift of her hands.

Resignation in his eyes now. *You owe me*, he mouthed, and helped Erica to a chair.

One away from all the computer interfaces, Liane noted. *Damn, he's* sharp.

Martin got Erica settled. Asked her polite, companionable questions about her life with his father. The usual *how did you meet*, however, quickly became a much more pointed 'Well, you sound like you were happy together. Why'd Dad ask you to leave?'

Erica's face shut down. She managed to reply, guiltily, 'He found that I hadn't had the Sensorium chips removed when I moved here. I'd just had them deactivated, and the external ports removed. I didn't think it would be such a big deal, but he acted as if I'd smuggled in vials of smallpox or something.' She straightened up, wiping at her face. 'I'll . . . head back over to my habitat, I suppose.'

'I'd tell you not to leave town,' Liane put in mildly. 'But it's not like you can.'

Erica sent her a poisonous glance, then headed out the airlock.

'Interesting,' Martin said as the door closed, 'that she never asked who was on your suspect list.'

'Isn't it, though.' Liane stared at the door. 'You didn't say much once you pulled her string.'

'I'm an actor. It's impolite to upstage someone when they're having their moment in the spotlight.' He shook his head. 'Even when they're the worst actress you've ever seen.'

Liane's lips quirked. 'You noticed that.'

'I would have had to be standing on Titan not to notice that.'

'You'd make a good detective.'

'Doubt the officers who broke up my parties back in the day would agree.' He snorted. 'Did my best to pull up the role of Detective Ramirez from *A Hunter's Heart* to play the "good cop" bit, though.'

'I caught that.' She met his eyes. 'You're observant. What else did you notice?'

'That she supposedly spent last night with the chief financial officer for this colony.' He paused. 'And weren't we just talking about contracts not getting paid on time? Dad never wrote his own cheques. Guess this Vardah person was the one doing the books for him.'

Liane grinned tightly. 'You know what they say about investigations? Follow the money. In this case, not yours, but your dad's. And what was being done with it.'

Martin's eyebrows rose, and he nodded. 'Do we start with Vardah, then?'

'No, we start by turning Alice loose on the colony books. And checking into my own deputy's alibi for last night, so that

I can rule her out safely.' Her lips turned down at the corners. *Though . . . it would make sense. Damn it.*

'That will take time,' Alice chimed in from her wrist. 'Cross-checking with banks located on Earth will take over two hours for each query.'

'Better get started, Alice. Spread the net over everything Vardah touched for Mr Donovan. Operational budget. The ecological preserve foundation. All of it. And send a note to Oluwusi. Tell him, in his copious spare time between dealing with angry tourists, to backcheck Teresa Chuquisengo's whereabouts last night. *Quietly*, since she's probably standing next to him, doing the same thankless job.' Liane paused, cocking a glance at Martin. 'How'd Erica get in the door?'

Martin stopped moving, thoughts flickering over his face. 'Dad would've denied her lock code access if he was throwing her out. Damn. She waltzed right in here, and I didn't even catch it.'

Liane nodded. 'Which means that somehow, her lock code still works. Though there's no record of her accessing the place last night. Still, if her alibi doesn't check out, she had motive and opportunity. Means? Remains to be seen.' She drummed her fingers against a tabletop. 'I don't really see her as a computer security expert. And she wasn't involved in colonial finances. Doesn't mean she couldn't have had help.'

Martin regarded her, his expression taut. 'What's the next step?'

Liane marshalled her thoughts. 'I go talk with your buddy Claude from the tram. He might know a few things. He had a meeting scheduled with your dad today, after all.' She fastened her helmet back in place. 'You want to come along, or do you want to keep listening to the letters?' Carefully casual. *God knows how I can protect him if he* doesn't *tag along. I can't put Teresa on him. Oluwusi is up to his neck in tasks I've already assigned him. And there's only one of me.*

'What Dad had to say has waited this long. It'll keep.' Martin followed her out the airlock, pausing as she reset the lock codes to keep people like Erica out. 'He said something about the carrying capacity of the heart. Funny that he never seemed to have much space there for me, but he could be worried about the whole human race.' He snorted. 'Wonder what made him think he could play god here, when he couldn't keep his own kid from screwing up.'

She sighed. 'People are complicated. I'm sure he cared. He just had a particularly lousy way of showing it. Dads can be like that. But . . . I saw how much he cared about your mom. And at the funeral, he looked lost. Like he was looking around for someone.' Her throat closed.

'You were there?' She saw his shoulders slump inside the suit. As if he were, once again, kicking himself for not having been there.

She tried to pass it off. 'Yeah. Senior officers let me attend, at his request.'

'He *asked* for you. And he asked you to come here, too.' Martin gave her a sudden piercing stare. 'But you've never been *with* him.'

Liane grimaced. It was a familiar question, unfortunately. 'God, no. It's . . . I broke the case. Not to put down the work of my senior officers. I just happened to luck into asking the right questions.' She looked away. She hated talking about it, particularly to someone so deeply *involved* in a case. 'And a few years later, when I'd worked enough other homicides that I didn't want to see another dead body, I reached out to your dad. I'd been reading some of his sociological stuff. He wound up asking me if my heart had been diminished. Said he didn't want to see modern life take another victim in me, and asked me here.' A helpless shrug. 'We can talk more about it later, if you like.'

A slow nod. 'That, and about my mom,' Martin said, his voice hollow.

'Not unless you really want to,' Liane replied tightly. 'I don't want to open up old wounds for you. Not when there's . . . all this in front of you to handle.'

Another nod as they stood, balancing outside the habitat, boots interlocked on opposite sides of the swaying, carbon fibre ropes. Ready to kick off and fly-swim away. Refracted sunlight poured through the dome above them, casting diamond shadows on the land below.

'I used to love this part,' Liane said out loud. 'The hunt. The chase. Feeling like you've got it all at your fingertips.' Part of her, if she were honest, still longed for that thrill. For the adrenal surge that came from it all, in that perfect moment where you could see all the possibilities unfolding, like the world in the crater below her feet.

After a long moment, Martin asked, 'So, which way are we going?'

'Let's go talk with Claude. Alice, is Claude Bensoussan at the hotel?'

A pause. 'No,' the AI replied. 'He is with Asim Qadir in the biology laboratory. Intersection of Dragomir Arch and Gages Ring.'

'Great,' Liane muttered. *And two lines of investigation decide to intersect there, too.* 'Let's go talk to them both, then.'

As he took off, she carefully drifted alongside. Partially to guide him, certainly. But also keeping a light orbit around him. Watching the other passers-by on the ropelines around them. Keeping her body interposed between him and them, as best she could—or at least cutting down on the angles of approach. *The killer didn't murder Donovan with a gun*, she told herself, working through the problem. *That doesn't mean that they don't have one. And if they had reason to kill him, they might well have reason to kill his son, too. Think, Liane. The person who did this doesn't have your training. They probably don't know how to use a rifle. They're not going to snipe him. Plus, poisoners don't usually change MO to guns unless they have no other choice.*

Drifting over the landscape below like clouds, her thoughts racing like a wind this domed environment would never experience. *No, this person likes to try to pass unseen, unnoticed, but does it from up close. If it happens again, it'll happen up close. Maybe a pistol at most. More likely a knife or poison again. Keep the situation contained. Keep yourself between him and anyone you genuinely suspect.*

God, Ben, why didn't you let me hire more guards?

Chapter Four

The laboratory proved to be another cluster of spherical habitats joined together, this time further from Amalthea's slopes. Surprisingly, it was far larger than his father's house. *Dad had his priorities*, Martin thought, obscurely proud of his father. *Who'd have thought it?*

Inside, he shook hands with Dr Asim Qadir, who had liquid dark eyes and a short, bristling beard that hinted at Moroccan ancestry. They'd found the scientist in his office, feet up on his desk, talking with, yes, Claude Bensoussan. The man now had his helmet off, unlike on the tram, giving Martin a better chance to examine his features. *French Algerian*, Martin thought, remembering what little Liane had disclosed from her files on the way over. *Radical in college. Then again, who isn't?* 'Nice to meet you again, Claude,' he remarked as the Security Chief pulled Dr Qadir over to the side to speak with him in a low, urgent voice.

Claude turned to stare at him for a long moment, and then recognition flared in his eyes. 'Fuck me,' he muttered. 'You're his *son*.'

Martin shrugged. 'I won't make a thing of it if you don't,' he offered as Liane came back over with Qadir. The scientist looked a little grey under the healthy olive tones of his skin. With a glance at Liane for permission, Martin turned towards Claude and asked affably, 'Could you check your bank finances? I had a report this morning that I'd somehow turned over ten thousand hydrogen credits to you. I don't mind donating to good causes, but I prefer to *know* when I'm doing it.'

Claude's face flushed. 'Are you calling me a thief?'

'No,' Liane interposed quietly. 'The credit transfer raised a red flag for both you and him, and I'd like to clear it up.'

'Well, I certainly didn't *steal* from him,' Claude huffed, pulling up his banking records on his wrist. At which point he frowned, staring at the information on the wide panel attached to his suit. 'Wait. This doesn't make sense.'

Liane stepped closer. 'May I see? It'll only confirm what we saw in Mr Donovan's records.'

Claude's face darkened almost to purple, a vein throbbing in his forehead. 'I am being *set up*,' he snarled. 'I have a meeting today with Benjamin Donovan, Sr., and someone is trying to discredit me—'

'He's dead,' Liane said, her words cutting Claude off mid-sentence. 'Mr Donovan was murdered last night. Someone isn't setting you up to discredit you or the unionising workers you represent. They're trying to suggest that Martin hired you and your organisation to help murder his father.'

Claude sat down very carefully in one of the chairs bolted into the lab's floor. *They probably secure the furniture around here so it doesn't bounce all over if you errantly brush past it while walking,* Martin thought. All of his thoughts had an absent quality right now, he noticed. A distance, as if he were just observing himself moving around, talking, thinking, acting. As if he stood on a stage the size of a planet. *Well, don't we all?*

'I'm not involved in anything like that. Mr Donovan was our best chance at getting the other corporations here on Vesta and out in the belt to *listen* to us. He had money and clout, and everything he's doing here is *supposedly* for the common good. Why would I kill him? It'd be like killing the proverbial golden goose,' Claude told Liane, his voice shaking. 'I'd . . . also like to contact my lawyer.'

'I'm not charging you with anything,' Liane replied calmly. 'Not that we have judges here. Best we have is an ombudsman who largely arbitrates interpersonal disputes and notarises documents. Li Hua is a great clerk, but I'm going to have to walk her through Alice's forensic accounting stuff by hand once I've got all my ducks in a row.' She paused. 'Mr Bensoussan. You weren't here till this morning. The handful of known HaveNot affiliates here in the preserve were nowhere near Mr Donovan's house last night.' She turned and gave Qadir a dour glance. 'Of course, *you* are an affiliate, Dr Qadir. And your greencams went down right when we needed to see what was going on in the preserve.' She shrugged, clearly examining the scientist's face.

Qadir's face flickered. 'I was the one who reported that to *you*, Chief.' A sharp frown. 'Given my history with the authorities in my homeland, I don't appreciate even the implicit threat.'

'I know.' Her voice remained rock-steady. 'But you wouldn't believe the number of times that the killer is the one who reports the crime.' She sighed. 'Not that I'm charging you, either, Asim, so don't look like that. Go ahead and give Mr Bensoussan comm access, so he can call his lawyer. And while we're all waiting for *that* call to reach Earth, to be heard, and for someone there to call him back . . . ' She paused.

'I'm far more interested in something else. Martin here tells me you talked with him about some unpaid contracts here in the nature preserve, Mr Bensoussan. Can you give me some details about that?'

Claude's mouth opened. Closed. 'You're interested in *that*?' he asked, sounding incredulous. 'One of the wealthiest men in the solar system is dead, and you're asking me about missed payments on a minor contract?'

Liane smiled. 'Details matter. Humour me. And then we'll turn my AI and her forensic accounting subroutines loose on that, too.'

Martin found his attention wandering. The pecuniary details weren't particularly engrossing—missed payments, promises of getting caught up, missed shipments by other contractors that also had turned out to be for reasons of late payment, specific dates . . . it all became a blur. So, he settled into a chair nearby and watched Dr Qadir working at a screen, touching and swiping on various camera feeds from the growing forest below. Fleeting impressions of tigers, racing up vertical trunks, bounding like squirrels from branch to branch and then gone, disguised once more. Herds of deer grazing both on the forest floor and among the branches. *Wonder what evolution's going to do to them, over time. An entirely arboreal ecosystem, with damn near no weight constraints. How fragile will their bones become, in twenty generations—not that it will matter, here. . .*

He cleared his throat, and Qadir looked up. 'Yes, Mr Donovan?'

'Martin, please. I wanted to ask how it is that you knew Mr Bensoussan. Why'd he come to you, of all the people on the station?' Martin figured he'd let Liane ask the hard questions.

Like, *how's your supply of incredibly costly insulin, imported from Earth?*

Qadir smiled briefly, an embarrassed expression. 'We went to university together, back on Earth. Participated in the Berber Awakening—you probably aren't aware of it, but the Berber language, culture, and lifeways have been under enormous pressure for centuries by Arabisation. We both thought that was unfair. And we were . . . close. Close in a way that an imam would have disapproved of.' He sighed, looking away, and Martin didn't push.

After a moment, Qadir continued. 'Going to rallies and such got us both pegged as radicals, and the threat of jail time was enough to push us onto different paths.' He shrugged. 'I shifted focus to ecosystem engineering in the face of Earth's climate crisis. He wound up in robotics. Time's a river that will push you this way and that. And sometimes, you wind up back on the shore beside someone you once knew, and it's . . . a wondrous thing to revisit your youth.' His dark eyes flicked to Bensoussan. 'And those once dear to you in it.' His shoulders slumped. 'He wouldn't have gotten on Mr Donovan's schedule without my assistance.'

There was a word coined centuries ago by a poet, Martin knew, that meant *the sudden realisation that everyone you meet has a life hidden from you.* He couldn't remember the word itself, but the sudden pressing sense of it rose up in him, seeing the expression on Qadir's face now. 'And your life here?' he asked, changing the subject. 'What does your job entail?'

'Oh, what don't I do?' Qadir chuckled, clearly relieved to be leaving the subject behind. 'I handle the nitrogen/oxygen balance of the air, particularly what comes out of our dome-level hydroponic farms. The structure of the soils we're building on the ground. The intricacies of the ecosystems in each biome. The overall carrying capacity of the preserve.' A smile spread across his face. 'I am a well-contented lab rat, Mr Donovan.'

Martin blinked. 'You talked with my father about his rat paradise.'

Qadir laughed. 'Many times! Here, I have meaningful work. Work that will last beyond my own lifetime. As far as I am concerned, this *is* paradise.'

Doesn't sound like he's got a motive to kill my dad, Martin thought, waves of blank exhaustion starting to roll over him. *Though I guess Liane's the one who decides if he's worth investigating further. The greencams all going offline at once is* super *convenient, though.*

He spent the next hour listening to more of his father's letters, piped through his own AI into the speakers in his suit helmet. Staring into nothing. Wondering if there would be clues in his father's maunderings.

As he pulled on his helmet in the airlock of the lab, Martin asked Liane, 'You get enough information here?'

'Yeah, I think so. I checked with Qadir about his insulin. Sure enough, about a third of his supply is missing. That puts *his* life in danger, damn it. We're not due for a supply drop of medications for another month.' Liane's voice sounded tight. When we catch whoever it is, I kind of want to take *that* out of their hide, too.'

Martin wanted to say *get in line*, but it wasn't really his place. And then, he realised something else. 'You said *we*. When *we* catch the person.'

She paused, checking the area around them, as she had been doing all day. Eyes wide-seeing, not focused on anything in particular. 'Yeah. I guess I did.'

Martin couldn't help but feel oddly warmed by that. 'Don't suppose people *eat* on this asteroid, do they? I don't think I've had anything since the spaceport this morning.'

'Oh. *Crap*. It's almost six pm Zulu, isn't it? C'mon. Back to my office. We keep food there. And my deputies—all two of them—have had long, shitty days keeping people off the trams and generally keeping my comm channels from getting burned off by pissed-off tourists and locals.' She nodded towards the west, where the security station hung from one of the rings closer towards Amalthea's grey flank. 'I'll introduce you to them.'

'Did the one deputy's alibi check out?' Maybe he'd missed that detail, listening to the letters.

'So far, yeah. She's getting married in a month, and was actually at a sort of bachelorette party till close to two am Zulu.'

'You have those here?'

'Notable lack of strippers. Mostly just drinking and loud music. But there were multiple witnesses, and her friends poured her into bed in her habitat. She's apparently had a hangover all day, and Oluwusi says she's been *charming* to work with as a result.' He could hear the grin in her voice, which clearly faded as she added, 'Maybe by tomorrow morning Alice will have had enough comm traffic time to piece together the accounting puzzle for us. Give us better answers.'

She wasn't kidding about her deputies being tired. Isaiah Oluwusi, who'd been handling the tourists and newly-arrived contractors for her, looked exhausted, his dark eyes sunken. 'Long day,' he noted in his light Kenyan accent, accepting a bowl of freeze-dried kelp noodles with tofu chunks from Liane and heading to a sink to add water to reheat it in a microwave.

'*Really* long day,' Teresa Chuquisengo agreed with a groan, putting her head down on the desk. Martin didn't envy her the headache she still clearly had. Given her last name, she was probably Peruvian by birth, likely Inca by ancestry. Her long, dark hair had been pulled back in a braid, and her weathered face spoke of long days spent in the sunshine on Earth. 'I pulled all the transit records like you asked, Chief. There are only a couple of people from inside the colony who have tickets at the spaceport for passage to Luna. You get three guesses as to who they are.'

'Erica Jablonski,' Martin said, accepting a bowl of noodles from Liane with a grateful nod. It might be rabbit food, but it smelled great, and *anything* solid in his stomach would stop the growling.

'That's a given,' Chuquisengo replied, leaning back and rubbing at her temples. 'Come on. Think bigger.'

'Vardah Parsamyan,' Liane returned, taking a seat at the table herself now, lightly blowing on her noodles to cool them.

'You take all the fun out of things by jumping to the end, Chief,' Oluwusi complained, grabbing a fork himself.

'You checked your insulin supply?' Liane asked Chuquisengo, ignoring the by-play.

'Locked up tight. I keep my habitat security protocols updated. My guess is that Dr Qadir doesn't.'

Martin just ate quietly, listening. Not imposing himself on them.

'Thing is,' Oluwusi pointed out quietly, 'So far, almost everything that's been done, *could've* been done just by password theft. Getting in and out of Dr Qadir's habitat with his insulin. Turning off the greencams. Clearing out Mr Donovan's files.'

'But not turning off his security and medical protocols. Or the vid cams up here outside the habitats, which are under *my* protocols.' Liane sounded particularly irritated by the latter.

Oluwusi shrugged. 'I did say *almost* everything. Not all of it.'

Liane tapped her fork against her bowl lightly. 'I think we've got most of the pieces together. Other than, well. Motive.' She sighed. 'I'll want to question Vardah in the morning. And I'll probably want both of you with me, to make it nice and formal.' She glanced at Martin. 'Probably best that you *don't* come along for that one.'

'Oh?' He continued eating mechanically.

'Yeah.' She exhaled. 'I think we're zeroing in on the whole "who done it" part, and the shock and numbness thing is going to wear off when you get some sleep tonight. You'll be into the anger part of the grieving process by the time you wake up, and I don't want to have to pry your hands from around her neck. Particularly if I'm wrong and Vardah has nothing to do with the murder.' A brief smile, like bitter winter. 'I'd like to be responsible about this.'

It all sounded logical. Reasonable. And yet, there was something that suggested Liane wasn't telling the whole truth. Martin frowned. 'I'll behave. I'll stand behind your deputies and not say a word.' He raised a hand as Liane started to reply. 'I've come this far. Let me see it through. Even if you only let me stand in the habitat's airlock.'

He watched her eyes flick to her deputies. Communicating with them without words, in the way in which people who'd long worked together did. He caught the way Oluwusi nodded, the way his eyes flicked towards Martin himself. Saying silently, *I'll take care of him, boss.*

But only when Liane nodded did Martin exhale.

Another mechanical bite. Another mechanical swallow. 'I've been listening to my dad's letters all day,' Martin said into the silence that pooled around him now. 'He still hasn't gotten around to explaining why he wanted me here. Just rats and carrying capacity and finding ways to make people's lives worth living. New modalities for community. A lot of stuff about how Western society has put primacy on the individual for so long that it's damaged us. Too much ego, not enough super-ego. That other societies inject more of a social-self into their people, a sense of *we-is-more-important-than-me*, and those of us from the West reject that, to our detriment. All *big ideas*. Nothing . . . personal.' He glanced across the table at Liane. 'When my mom died—' The room somehow went even quieter. Just the hiss of the air recycling system in the background now. '—I couldn't make myself read the reports. Not even after I got out of rehab. So, I know Jacob Itzal wound up confessing to her murder. Life imprisonment, up for parole in like, five years now, or something. But not motives.' He stared at the bottom of the bowl, noting the fractal patterns in the glaze.

Like all the paths of a life not yet taken.

Martin swallowed and forced himself to go on. 'I wanted to know *why*. But I also . . . I couldn't. I'd just gotten my head back together after rehab. Reading about the why and the how felt like I'd just strap myself to an anchor and sink back down again.'

Dimly, he noted that both deputies were quickly picking up their bowls and heading for the sink. Leaving the two of them to as much privacy, as much psychic space, as could be managed in the small office.

Liane nodded, sitting up. 'Yeah,' she said, with so much empathy in her voice that Martin's throat suddenly ached. 'I get that. And right now, it's all probably coming back up for you, because of all this.' She sighed. 'Come on. Let's go someplace with a better view, and I'll tell you as much as you can stand to hear.'

The place with a better view turned out to be her private quarters, in a bubble above the office. About the size of a studio apartment, it had a bed, kitchen, and hygiene facilities all in one. *Spartan* described it better than cosy. But it did, in fact, have a floor-to-ceiling window panel.

'Ever feel like you're going to fall out?' Martin asked, unsure of where to sit.

Liane gestured him towards the room's single chair, another swinging net contraption, while taking a seat at the edge of her bed, which was firmly secured to the floor. 'Every day,' she replied, glancing at the window. 'But it reminds me that I'm *here*, so I like it. Yeah. I'm another contented rat in your dad's paradise.' She held up a finger to forestall any retort. 'You asked about your mom's murderer.'

Martin felt all the words inside him wither and die. He simply sat where indicated and nodded. Listening.

'It's probably not purely a modern thing,' Liane began, a little haltingly, 'but it's definitely more of a modern tendency than a universal one. For people to project themselves into a relationship. To see more than is there. Jacob Itzal had a really crappy relationship with his own father. Felt rejected at every turn. Like too much was demanded or expected. But he did well in school. Top marks, top honours. When he came to work for your dad at Sensorium, he started off in chip architecture and design. Got your dad's attention for his brilliance. Got brought onto the CEO's team, still in his twenties. I mean, hell, he's your age, Martin.' Her lips turned down.

Martin absorbed that. 'And when my dad said he liked what Jacob was doing, praised his work—I mean, I have to *assume* he occasionally praised people. I was never on the receiving end, but people have this odd, steadfast loyalty to my father that's inexplicable *without* that—' a direct glance at her, for her own steadfast loyalties, and he had the satisfaction of watching her light shrug of rueful, self-aware acknowledgement. 'Jacob found himself a father figure to replace his own.'

Liane sighed. 'Yeah. But like I said earlier today, people are complicated. I think he thought that your father loved him. Like a son. Your father probably expressed some disappointment in you. And Jacob . . . saw more than was there. He also harboured some romantic fantasies about your dad that were probably not all that healthy. And when your dad came down on him one week, threatened to fire him over a minor mistake . . . it also happened to be the week that your father had commented that he hoped you'd be getting out of rehab and maybe coming home for a visit. . . ' She shrugged. 'Delusional people make the same stupid choices the rest of us do.'

And yet, there was compassion in her voice. For all of them, maybe.

Martin grimaced. 'So why kill my *mom*?' He could almost wrap his head around it. Like a character he was going to play. But knowing the people involved made it almost impossible to work out in his mind. 'That wasn't going to suddenly change *everything* for him. It wasn't going to make my dad love him. I mean, *maybe* he'd be more dependent on him, but. . .'

'Because your mom wasn't the target.' Soft, quiet words. 'The senior detectives considered that your dad might have been the target, since, you know. Public figure, controversial, responsible for Sensorium tech, all of that . . . but it seemed so specific. Gunshot through the window of her car, close range. And she'd spoken out, as a medical doctor, on some controversial issues, herself, recently. Had expressed a desire to run for office to address those healthcare issues. So, they figured she was the actual target.'

'You didn't agree.' It wasn't a question.

'She wasn't supposed to be in the car. He was supposed to have been heading to a conference. But he got sick that morning and your mom offered to read his speech for him. The AI shuttled her along the scheduled route, and Jacob took a hasty shot without confirming his target.'

After a moment, he asked dully, 'How'd you figure it out?'

'Jacob was just . . . so upset. The plan had never been to kill your mom. Just to . . . take out his rage on your dad, I guess. At him. The world. At all his broken dreams. I'd flagged him as a person of interest, because he'd gotten a write-up with HR over the whole threat-of-firing and the very loud argument he'd gotten into with your father over it. I swung back around to talk to him a few times. I was sympathetic and I listened, and eventually, he started making mistakes.' A faint shrug.

'Good cop.'

'Nah. Just a cop who *listened*,' Liane corrected. 'It's supposed to be in the job description, believe it or not. Your father told me it was my compassion that made me good at my job. And that it would be what would destroy me if I stayed in the job too long. He had a really annoying tendency to be right sometimes.'

Martin looked at the floor. 'Yeah.' *Just not right about me. Except when he was.*

'I should get you back over to your father's habitat,' Liane noted, sounding reluctant. 'It's late.'

'And anyone who killed my father could have motive to kill me, depending on the contents of his will,' Martin pointed out, catching the arrested look on her face. 'Which I expect his lawyers on Earth have in hand, and they're probably getting the executor and all the other necessary ducks in a row. That's why you've "let" me tag along with you today. You don't have the manpower to put a twenty-four hour guard on me. Besides yourself.' Martin paused, and then gave her a crooked grin. 'Didn't expect me to put that one together?'

Liane sighed, raising her hands in surrender. 'I was trying to be subtle about the bodyguarding. You strike me as the type who doesn't like being nursemaided.'

'I've had bodyguards on me since my first major Sensorium release. You wouldn't believe how many people think that because they *think* they've touched you in sim, they have every right to touch you in person.' He caught the way her eyes flickered with almost comical apprehension and added, 'You've given me a remarkable amount of personal space. You're fine.' A pause. 'So, if you're trying to find a polite way to keep me in arm's reach tonight without throwing your virtue to the winds, I expect this weird hanging chair of yours turns into a hammock, right?' He pointed at the curving walls. 'And those are a lot more solid than they look, right? As in, unlikely to pop?'

She blinked, bemused and off guard. "Yeah. The walls are basically bulletproof from the outside. From the inside, not so much, but from the outside, they have to be able to resist any micro-meteor debris since they're our last line of defence.' She paused. 'You're making this way easier than I thought it would

train stations. They picked their kids up in their arms and stepped right out onto the tracks with an L train barrelling down at them.'

'Jesus,' Martin muttered.

'Yeah.' Her voice had shifted. Raw pain now. 'I got to identify the bodies. Mothers and children. I'd done everything I could. I'd talked them into *leaving* the cult. But the cult never left their heads. I guess the moms thought they'd betrayed the rest of the people they were with, by leaving before it all blew up. They couldn't leave that part of their identity behind. Become part of any other *we*. So, I read a lot of sociology stuff. Wound up writing your dad. Asking how the *fuck* society has gotten so messed up that any one of us could just . . . do that.'

'Did he have answers for you?' Martin asked. He didn't know what to do. If he'd known her for longer than a day, he'd have stood. Gone to her. Offered to wrap his arms around her. But the newness of their acquaintance suggested that he should just stay put.

'No. He said he was looking for them, though. And I was welcome to come help. Or just stay someplace safe till I could put my head back together. But that I'd need to earn my keep.'

'Forgive me, but what differentiates my dad's little paradise from that cult? None of you can leave. Not really, once you've adjusted to the gravity. Not without a lot of physical therapy in stronger gravity, anyway.' Martin tried not to sound sarcastic. He had too much respect for Liane by now—for the compassion of her heart, for the acuity of her mind—for that.

'Your dad never said that he has all the answers. Whenever one of us here came up with a different idea, if he thought it was better than his own, he'd incorporate it. And none of us came here as wide-eyed kids seeking wisdom from a guru.

We're older. Stable personalities. I still write to my parents every week. We're not cut off from a larger community.'

Martin nodded, lying back. 'Thank you for telling me,' he finally said. 'Seems a crap way to express gratitude for someone baring their soul. But thank you.'

'It's not much of a bedtime story,' Liane replied, sounding exhausted. 'But it's what I've got. Get some sleep, alright?'

Chapter Five

Vardah Parsamyan pursed her lips and stared at Erica, who'd curled up in a soft, round chair at the centre of her living space. 'You weren't supposed to go back there,' she muttered darkly. 'You couldn't just . . . leave? Quietly?' *You injected yourself right into the middle of the damn investigation.*

Erica waved a hand, looking distraught. 'I didn't know he was *dead*. I figured I'd take one more shot at patching things up. He could be affectionate, in his way.' A sidelong glance at Vardah. Knowing that those words wouldn't go over well with the woman who'd become her lover on the side.

Vardah ground her teeth. Erica could be so obstinately self-centred. But she settled down on the chair beside her and rested an arm around her shoulders. 'You don't *need* him,' she pointed out in a tone of sweet reason. 'He was controlling. He didn't want you using the Sensorium, which is just hypocritical, since he *created* the damn thing, right?' Step by patient step. Walking Erica back over the whole path, once again. 'He hardly paid you any attention in the past nine months. Locked in on bringing his wayward son home again.' She ran her fingers through Erica's frosted hair. 'Which had the side benefit of letting *us* get to know each other. And I plan to take care of you better than he ever did. All we need to do is *leave*.'

And the funds she'd been steadily embezzling from the colony's foundation and operational budget for the past two years would ensure she'd have a wonderful life ahead of her.

With or without Erica.

Without was totally an option, if Erica persisted in being melodramatic. It wouldn't even be all that difficult to flip all the evidence she'd planted so far to point at Donovan's son to point at Erica instead. *So stop being stupid. He's dead. You shouldn't even be sorry about it, the way he treated you.* 'He barely talked to you. Treated you like a mannequin.' Gentle, chiding tone. Erica could be manipulated. You just had to go at it carefully.

Erica raised her face. Up close, Vardah could just see the tiny crow's feet around her red-rimmed eyes. Signs of aging that no amount of plastic surgery could efface. 'Where *were* you last night?' she demanded. 'I told the security chief that you were helping me pack. But you weren't.'

Vardah went still, trying to ascertain if that was, somehow, a *threat*. She forced a laugh past her tightening throat. 'How would you know if I were or not? You fell asleep after a bottle of wine, darling.'

Erica pulled away from Vardah. 'I covered for you,' she growled, suddenly far more assertive than she'd ever been. 'So please do not fucking tell me that I'm an accessory *after the fact* now.' She folded her arms over her chest, glaring at Vardah. 'Where *were* you? *My* habitat records weren't wiped. They say you left after midnight Zulu and didn't get back till nearly two.'

Shit, Vardah thought blankly. 'I went out for some air. Nothing more dramatic than that.'

'Don't you *lie*. I won't be used anymore. Not by him, and not by you! I am *done* with being used!'

Vardah slapped her, leaving a red welt across her cheek. Deep inside her hand, fragile bones protested. 'What do you know about being *used*?' Vardah snapped. 'I'm the one who's been here from the beginning. Watching my bones turn to snowflakes. Always with the promise hinted at, that if I bought into the dream, worked hard enough, I'd be appointed— anointed!—Donovan's successor. I can't remember a time when he *wasn't* talking about stepping down and letting someone else take over. And who else was it going to be, but *me*? The one who made all his little dreams of paradise come true, managed all the money so he could play *god*.' She wanted to spit. 'Then you came along and we *got acquainted* because you were bored and I was lonely. He found out about us, and you know what else happened? He started looking at the books a little more carefully.'

Erica backed towards the airlock, her face turning ashen. 'Oh my god. You *did* kill him.'

'He was going to kick us both out. Leave us without even the means to put our bodies back together on Mars or Luna. You know how much time and money it takes to rehab yourself for Earth gravity after *five years* on this rock? About another five years, *darling*.' Vardah's hands clenched and unclenched. It hadn't been hard to get Donovan's passwords. They were all for the internal network that her operations team oversaw anyway. And setting up cash transactions between his son and a random HaveNot representative? Only a little harder, when you ran the finances for a major corporation that owned a bank as a subsidiary.

No, the hardest part had been going through with it. She'd

stood there in his bedroom for a long time, watching him sleep, before finally nerving herself to push the needle into his arm. Not her own insulin, of course. She couldn't risk her own life any further than she already was. And she'd gotten the shakes and nausea afterwards, even as she hefted his body, so startlingly light in the microgravity, onto her shoulders for disposal. *You deserved it,* she'd kept thinking silently as she went through each step of her meticulous plan, erasing video records and setting a worm to devour data on his file system. *You did.*

'I—but why would the books . . . You were *stealing* from him?' Erica sounded so baffled, and it just made Vardah's anger worse. The snivelling tone, the pleading to *understand*, when she should damned well be grateful. 'Why?'

Because he deserved it! Vardah wanted to shout. *Because he stole my life under false pretences! I was never going to get what I deserved. He was just waiting all this time to bring his precious parasitical son back—*

Which was when the airlock door chimed, and a voice came through the annunciator. 'Ms Jablonski? This is Security Chief Sheridan. If Ms Parsamyan is with you, I'd like a word with her regarding the embezzlement of colonial funds and her whereabouts the night before last.'

'I am *not* going to jail with you,' Erica told Vardah, her voice shrill, and lunged for the airlock door.

Vardah launched herself at Erica. The result wasn't the satisfying crunch it would have been on Earth, but a slow tumble of limbs towards the floor. She managed to get her hands wrapped in Erica's hair, and as she watched those red lips encircle a scream, she brought the other woman's head down on the edge of a coffee table.

And then Vardah released the suddenly-limp form and stumbled backwards, shaking. She hadn't meant to do that. This wasn't in the plan. The plan was to just get to the spaceport, where the resupply ship, the one that had brought Donovan's son yesterday, was refuelling for the trip back to Luna.

All Erica had needed to do was keep her mouth *shut*.

'Now look what you made me do,' Vardah whispered, her hands shaking.

The airlock pinged again. 'Ms Jablonski? Are you alright?'

Vardah's eyes flicked to Erica's body. *Not dead yet. Otherwise the monitors would be screaming. I have time to do something. But what?*

Her eyes fell on the kitchen knives, and the thin walls of the habitat. Like steel on the outside; like a soap bubble on the interior. *I am not going down. And if I do, I'm not going alone.*

Chapter Six

Martin had been balancing outside, feeling like he was getting the hang of life here in low gravity. One hand looped lightly along one of the high ropes, feet aligned on a lower strand. Watching Liane and her deputies, all wearing tactical gear that they'd clearly pulled out of storage for the first time in colonial history. 'Ms Jablonski?' Liane tried again, and then began to punch in an override code at the door.

Which was when something moved at the periphery of Martin's vision, and he had enough time to turn his head to see a woman's shape gliding towards him from the side of the habitat sphere. Almost comical slow motion. *Like an attack in a fishbowl,* Martin thought, raising a hand to ward her off—

—which was when the attacker raised a taser and fired the electrodes at him. They pierced through his suit, and the shock threw him backwards, off the rope—

—falling in a daze, feeling the agony of the voltage fade as a body thudded into his. Whirl of straining hoverblade motors, feel of something sharp pressing into his suit. A trickle of his own blood—*hey, Sensorium vids never got that right, it's surprisingly cold*—

—seeing Liane and her deputies hovering above them like

angels. Spreading out. Dim awareness returning as the person holding him up, knife at his throat, started issuing demands, 'You're going to let me get on that tram with him. I'll take him with me to the spaceport as insurance—'

'Hey, I'm willing to work with you.' He could hear strain behind the calmness in Liane's voice. *Wonder if she trained as a negotiator? I better hope she did. . .*

'But you're improvising, aren't you?' Oluwusi put in, obviously trying to move Vardah's attention to him. 'Trying to take him as a hostage, what, all the way back to Earth? It's a year's trip. You'll have to sleep sometime. Eat. Let your guard down. And then what?'

Too fast, Martin realised, wanting to shake his head, but the knife at his throat forbade movement. *They need to get her to relax, not make her more tense—wait. What's that?*

Vardah had shifted him around to face Oluwusi. But out of the corner of his eyes, he could see a dozen tiny drones pop out from behind Liane. *Oh, shit. If those are the shock drones she says she saves for tigers, and if they zap Vardah while she's holding me. . . this is going to* hurt—

The knife pulled away from his throat for an instant as Vardah spotted the drones too, and Martin leaned away from the blade. Braced himself …

… And screamed from behind his own clenched teeth as he and Vardah once again began to fall.

*

Liane watched the two entangled figures drop. She swore, realising that her shock drones had shorted out the flight capabilities of Vardah's suit, and dropped into a diving posture before arrowing down towards them. Their limbs, spread, caught the air as they tumbled. Her body, positioned like a knife, cut through the air without resistance. *Come on. Come on. Just a couple more metres—*

She got a fingertip on one of Martin's flailing arms. Slid her hand around his wrist, and apologised to him mentally for the potential dislocation before yanking him up towards her while kicking in her own suit's hoverblades once more.

And then swore again as both he *and* Vardah, still somehow holding onto him, flew up past her, like a whip made of flesh. Come *on*!' Liane shouted to an uncaring universe. 'Give me a break!'

Martin must have regained consciousness, because his body spasmed, and he started fighting. Hard. He had a body still accustomed to full Earth gravity, a body that had *worked* for its muscle and tone. A body that knew how to kick.

Vardah spun away in a parabolic arc, slowly tumbling towards the forest where she'd left Benjamin Donovan, Sr.'s body. Air hoses torn and dangling, she'd probably have hypoxia by the time she landed. If she survived the fall—Liane didn't give her good chances of survival.

But for the moment, her job wasn't chasing the suspect. It was keeping Martin alive. So, she moved in. Wrapped her arms around his struggling form. Not a full pin, but a kind of demented *pas de deux* mid-air. 'Hey!' she shouted. 'Hey! It's me! It's alright!'

For a wonder, he stopped fighting. But as his head slumped forward, Liane could see that his air tubes, too, had been compromised. 'Got to get you to the doctor,' she muttered. 'Vardah can wait.'

Chapter Seven

'How do we delude ourselves?' Benjamin Donovan, Sr. asked, his hands clasped behind his back, staring up at a clear blue sky. An *Earth* sky. 'We think that everything we do is a choice. But it's not. Even our vaunted identities aren't entirely dictated by genetics or self-aware decisions. Much of who we think we are boils down to our environment. This new environment I've built here will work on the people and animals in it. Any latent viroids in the regolith will change the shape of our brains over time as our bodies adapt to them, and they to us.'

Martin groaned. 'This again, Dad?' He leaned back, against a tree trunk. Warm sunshine filtered down through its leaves. 'That's a fucking horrible way to look at life. I *refuse* to believe that what we choose doesn't matter. Anything else is just . . . a coward's embrace of determinism. Giving up all responsibility for our own actions.'

'Of course you believe that. You've played a hero so often that you're conditioned to do so.'

Martin sighed. 'I know I'm not a hero. Heroes save other people. They don't need to have their own nuts pulled out of the fire, time and again. But I thought you'd actually *like* the concept of me not running away from my responsibilities. Of course, who am I kidding? You're dead.'

His father turned back towards him, exhaling a puff of white smoke. 'Yes, I am. Are you?'

Martin had a brief memory flash. Falling. Falling forever towards the implacable ground. 'Probably.'

His father shrugged. 'What you believe doesn't make something more or less true. There are billions of people out there who will refuse to believe that who they are isn't a matter of choice, of their own appetites, because the concept that we're all part of a greater community, a hive, that makes us into what we are will offend their concept of themselves as thinking, reasoning creatures utterly in control of their own destiny. But we're not. None of us are separate from the system. We're all products of it. Even me. And even you.'

Martin rubbed his eyes. 'That has got to be the world's best pot. You absolutely will not shut up once you get some of that in you. You should've smoked that more often when I was a kid.'

'Martin? Hush for a moment.' His father paused. 'This is me, trying to apologise. I was just as damaged by the environment and system as you were. Just in different ways. This place?' He gestured, and the blue sky faded into the black diamond latticework and milky white interior of the dome, 'was my apology. To you. To humanity. My last chance to make something better. I wanted you to see it. To participate in it. To become . . . better. I probably didn't say it very well in my letters. But that's what I *wanted* to say.'

Martin stared at him. 'That's the most words I've ever heard you say at once to my face.'

'That's because I'm not the one saying them. I'm dead, remember? This is you talking to yourself. Hallucinations brought on by hypoxia. For all you know, Liane is playing my letters to you to wake you up out of a coma.' His father exhaled. 'So, I'm saying what you think you need to hear.'

'So, I better say my lines and wake up?'

'Probably.'

'Goodbye, Dad. I love you. In spite of everything.'

He saw his father smile.

But then he faded away like smoke.

*

Martin's eyes opened as the beeping of medical equipment finally woke him. He swallowed past a dry throat and tried to sit up, feeling the prickle of an IV in his arm. *Whoa. Rehab flashbacks. Least I'm not strapped down.*

At his bedside, asleep in a chair, was Liane Sheridan. His stirring had roused her, though, and her own eyes opened now. 'Hey. You're awake.' She sat up. 'Head feel okay? Dr Hernandez says we got you on oxygen before the hypoxia could do much damage.'

'If I had brain damage . . . how would you be able to tell?' Martin's tongue felt thick. 'Given my history.'

Liane gave him the most annoyed look he'd gotten from any human since his last assistant had quit. 'I am going to beat you with your own pillows if you don't stop that,' she threatened.

'Not really sporting—least let me get this IV out first?' He managed a facsimile of a smile, and then winced. 'Wow. Please tell me the other guy looks at least as bad?' Memory filtered back. 'Oh. Wait. This is from being tased. Like, *twice*.'

She winced. 'Yeah. Sorry about that. I needed the knife away from your throat.'

He nodded, leaning back and closing his eyes. Listened as she noted that Vardah's body had been recovered from, yes, the tigers. That Erica was recovering, too, but would be sent back to Luna. Probably not to face charges as an accessory, but who knew, really?

None of that mattered right now.

'I know you haven't exactly had time to think about what you'll do, but you're about to have all your father's lawyers descend on you. Sole heir, all that.'

It wasn't even a choice. 'I'm staying here. He wanted to make this place a model for humanity. A better way to live. It's not a bad dream.' Martin coughed, and then glanced at her. 'Answer a question for me?'

'Sure.'

'Your heart. Think it's got the carrying capacity for one more stray here?' He reached out, offering her his hand.

Liane blinked. Smiled. And accepted his hand in hers. 'Let me get back to you on that.'

Martin closed his eyes again. He had time.

That, above all else, was his father's final legacy.

Discover Luna Novella in our store:

https://www.lunapresspublishing.com/shop

www.ingramcontent.com/pod-product-compliance
Ingram Content Group UK Ltd.
Pitfield, Milton Keynes, MK11 3LW, UK
UKHW040822100225
4520UKWH00029B/305